"Do you see the cat lady anywhere?" asked Sarah-Jane.

Timothy glanced around quickly. "Yes! She's looking all around—like she's hunting for someone in the crowd. Probably us."

He looked at the bored boy behind the table. "Somebody's following my cousins and me. Can we hide under your table?"

This looks like a case for the T.C.D.C.

THE MYSTERY OF THE
LAUGHING CAT

Elspeth Campbell Murphy
Illustrated by Chris Wold Dyrud

Chariot Books
David C. Cook Publishing Co.

A Wise Owl Book
Published by Chariot Books,
an imprint of David C. Cook Publishing Co.
David C. Cook Publishing Co., Elgin, Illinois 60120
David C. Cook Publishing Co., Weston, Ontario
Nova Distribution, Ltd., Torquay, England

The Mystery of the Laughing Cat
©1988 by Elspeth Campbell Murphy for text
and Chris Wold Dyrud for illustrations

Cover design by Chris Patchel
First Printing, 1988
Printed in the United States of America
95 94 93   10 9 8 7

Library of Congress Cataloging-in-Publication Data
Murphy, Elspeth Campbell.
    The mystery of the laughing cat.

    (The Ten Commandments mysteries)
    Summary: Three cousins pursue a thief at a flea market and learn
about the commandment "You shall not steal."
    [1. Cousins—Fiction. 2. Mystery and detective stories. 3. Ten
commandments—Fiction.]
I. Dyrud, Chris Wold, ill. II. Title. III. Series:
Murphy, Elspeth Campbell. Ten Commandments mysteries.
PZ7.M95316Myd   1988   [FIC]   87-16719
ISBN 1-55513-649-4

"You shall not steal."

Exodus 20:15 (NIV)

CONTENTS

"See?" said Sarah-Jane to her cousin Timothy and her other cousin Titus. "This is the flea market I was telling you about."

"Wow!" said Timothy. "Look at all this neat junk! It's like the biggest garage sale I ever saw!"

"EXcellent stuff!" said Titus.

The three cousins stood at one end of a very long building. The building was filled with lots of tables where dealers were selling all kinds of interesting things.

Sarah-Jane's father came up behind the cousins. He said, "I guess you kids aren't too interested in looking at antique furniture with us grown-ups. Anyway, we think you're old enough to be on your own for a while. What do you

9

think?''

"YES!!" they said together.

"All right, then. Listen up. Here are your three rules. Rule Number One: Stay in the building. Rule Number Two: Stay together. Rule Number Three: Be back here at exactly two o'clock.''

The cousins were all set to take off. But Sarah-Jane's father had another surprise for them. He gave them each three dollars. He said, ''This is your 'mad money.' You know, your 'blow bucks.' ''

Sarah-Jane asked, ''Do you mean we can use

the money to buy anything we want to here at the flea market?''

''Anything but fleas,'' said her father sternly. ''Your poor dog has enough fleas already.''

''Oh, Daddy,'' said Sarah-Jane.

''Thanks, Uncle Art!''

''Thanks, Uncle Art!''

''Yes, thank you, Daddy!''

''Remember the three rules!'' Sarah-Jane's dad called after them.

2
THE STOLEN COINS

Sarah-Jane lived in the country. Titus lived in the city. And Timothy lived in a suburb in between.

The cousins loved it when their families got together as they did today.

When Sarah-Jane said her prayers at night, she always said, "God bless Tim and Ti."

Titus always said, "God bless Tim and S-J."

And Timothy always said, "God bless Ti and S-J."

Today they had to stay together at the flea market. But that wasn't a hard rule to obey—because they *loved* being together.

Titus looked at the rows of tables. He said, "We need a plan for how to spend our time. I want to see if they have any neat, old comic books for sale."

Timothy said, "OK, Ti. I want to look for buttons to add to my collection. Maybe I can find some really unusual ones. How about you, S-J?"

"I don't know yet," said Sarah-Jane. "But let's go all the way down this long aisle here. Then we can cross over at the other end of the room and come back up the other long aisle. OK?"

The boys thought this was a good idea. So the three of them started off. About halfway down the aisle, they saw two policemen talking to one of the dealers.

The cousins got close enough to hear the old dealer say, "My *best coins* are gone! The thief took my *best rare coins*! They're worth a lot of money. What am I going to do?"

The dealer's assistant shook his head. He said to the police, "I just don't understand how this could have happened."

Sarah-Jane whispered to Timothy and Titus, "I think it's *mean* when people take other people's stuff."

The boys agreed with her. Titus said, "We're memorizing the Ten Commandments in Sunday school. One of them is 'You shall not steal.' ''

Sarah-Jane nodded. "My class hasn't started the Ten Commandments yet," she said. "But I know most of them already."

Timothy said, "I wish *everybody* knew them— and *obeyed* them. Because taking other people's stuff is wrong."

The police didn't want people getting in the way. So the three cousins moved along.

At the next table Sarah-Jane suddenly stopped. "Now I know *exactly* what I want to buy!" she said. "Sort of."

Timothy and Titus looked at her in surprise. The table was crammed full of vases and bottles and figurines. The boys didn't see anything they liked at all.

Sarah-Jane said, "I can't decide between the china flamingo and the china cat. No, wait a minute. I definitely want the cat."

"Are you crazy?" Titus muttered.

"It costs three dollars," added Timothy. "Are you going to spend your whole 'mad money' on *one thing*?"

"I *love* that cat!" said Sarah-Jane. "She has a

sweet little face. Look at the way she's smiling. It looks like she's laughing to herself. It's like she just told herself a joke. Or maybe she knows a secret.''

Timothy and Titus just looked at each other and shook their heads.

The saleslady picked up the cat from the table and said to Sarah-Jane, "Let me find you a bag."

Just then a young woman in a pink-checked blouse rushed up to the table. She got out her wallet and pointed to the cat in the saleslady's hands. "I want to buy that cat!" she said as if she were giving an order. "How much is it?"

"I'm sorry," said the saleslady. "But this cat has already been sold."

3
SOLD—TO SARAH-JANE

The young woman stared at the saleslady. "But that's impossible! I—I mean, I want it for my niece's birthday. I really must have it!"

"I'm sorry," said the saleslady more firmly. "But this little girl was here first. And I already sold the cat to her."

The young woman whirled around and looked hard at Sarah-Jane. She opened her mouth as if to say something. But instead she turned and stomped away.

"My goodness!" said the saleslady. "She certainly wanted this cat, didn't she? But now it belongs to you, my dear. I'm sorry I couldn't find a bag for you."

"That's OK," said Sarah-Jane. "I'd rather carry her without a bag. That way, it will be like

I'm cuddling her. She's such a sweet kitty."

Timothy and Titus looked at each other and rolled their eyes.

When the saleslady handed the cat to Sarah-Jane, there was a jingling sound.

Timothy said, "It sounds like there's something loose inside there!"

The saleslady said, "I'm not surprised. See this slot on the back of the cat's head? This is like a piggy bank—only it's a cat."

"Oh!" said Sarah-Jane. "That's nice! I didn't even know that when I picked it out." She turned the cat upside down and started to pull out the black rubber stopper. "I'd better give the money back to you."

But the saleslady smiled and said, "Oh, please don't bother. It's probably just some loose change. Consider it a bonus."

"Wow! Thank you!" said Sarah-Jane. She would have liked to talk to the saleslady some more. But Timothy and Titus were impatient to be off.

"Tell you what, Tim and Ti," Sarah-Jane said as she hurried along beside them. "After you buy your stuff, I'll open my cat bank. Then I'll split the extra money with you."

"Hey, great!" said Timothy.

"That's really nice of you, S-J," said Titus. Then he said, "I think I see some comic books. Come on! Over there at the end of this aisle."

But they hadn't gone very far when the young woman in the pink-checked blouse came up to them.

The woman smiled hard at Sarah-Jane and spoke in a sticky-sweet kind of voice. "Little girl, do you mind if I ask how much you paid for that cat?"

"Three dollars," said Sarah-Jane. She hugged the cat tighter.

The woman got out her wallet. "Well, I'll tell you what. I'll *double* that. I'll buy the cat from you for *six* dollars. How would that be?"

Timothy and Titus turned to Sarah-Jane. "Wow! Six dollars!"

But Sarah-Jane just shook her head. She used the same polite-but-firm voice the saleslady had used. "I'm sorry. But this cat is not for sale."

The woman sighed impatiently. "Now look here, kid. I haven't got all day. *I want to buy that cat!* I mean—well, you see, it's for my grandmother. She collects cats. And that one would be just right for her.''

But Sarah-Jane just shook her head harder. ''I don't want to sell it. I picked it out. I bought it with my own money. It belongs to me now.'' Then she clamped her lips shut tight.

The young woman grunted angrily. Then she shoved her wallet back into her purse and left without another word.

The cousins stared after her in surprise.

On their way to the comic books, Titus said, ''I wonder why that lady wants S-J's cat so much?''

''Yeah,'' said Timothy, grinning at Sarah-Jane. ''Why, would *anyone* want that cat?''

Sarah-Jane turned to him indignantly. ''Because it's a beautiful cat, that's why! It's a sweet little kitty with a very cute smile.'' Then Sarah-Jane added thoughtfully, ''Something funny is going on here. That woman told the saleslady she wanted the cat for her *niece*. But she told me she wanted it for her *grandmother*. I wonder why she *really* wants it?''

But they didn't have time to think about this,

because they had arrived at the comic books corner.

There were comic books everywhere! Spread out on tables. Piled on shelves. Even stacked on the floor.

Sarah-Jane set her cat carefully on the floor. Then she and Timothy helped Titus hunt for the kinds of comic books he wanted.

By the time they were done, their hands and faces were streaked with dust. But Titus was beaming. "These are *so EXcellent*!" he cried. "And I still have some change left."

Suddenly his smile faded. "S-J! Your cat! Look out!"

Sarah-Jane whirled around to see the woman in the pink-checked blouse *reaching* for the cat.

Timothy was closer, and he snatched it away just in time.

The woman scowled at them. "Why are you looking at me like that? I was only going to move the cat so it wouldn't get knocked over and broken. Some thanks I get for trying to be nice!"

And with that she hurried away.

Timothy handed the cat to Sarah-Jane. "You'd

better not set this down again, S-J!''

"Tim's right, S-J," said Titus. "I don't believe her story about moving the cat. I think she was trying to *steal* it, since you wouldn't sell it to her."

Sarah-Jane looked around. "Where did she go? I don't see her anymore."

"Maybe she gave up and left the flea market," said Titus.

"I sure hope so," said Sarah-Jane.

Timothy said, "Well, let's go see if I can find some unusual buttons for my collection."

5
THAT LADY AGAIN

A bored-looking older boy sat behind the button table. (He was taking care of things while his father went for lunch.) The boy was wearing a T-shirt that said *Joey* on it. "Can I help you?" he asked.

Timothy's eyes lit up when he saw the boxes and boxes and boxes of buttons.

Titus sighed and said to Sarah-Jane, "This could take awhile."

Timothy didn't need help picking out buttons. So Titus sat down on the floor, leaned against a post, and opened a comic book.

Sarah-Jane leaned against the post, too. But she stayed standing, just looking around the flea market.

Suddenly she gasped and ducked down beside

Titus.

Titus looked up from his comic book in surprise. "Hey, S-J! What's the matter? You have a funny look on your face."

"It's that lady again, Ti!" Sarah-Jane whispered. "I think she's following us. What should we do?"

"Hide till she goes away," said Titus. "We need to get Tim's attention. "Psst! Tim! Come to the end of the table. We're down here. No, don't look down. Just act natural."

"What's going on?" asked Timothy as he sorted through some buttons.

"Do you see that cat lady anywhere?" asked Sarah-Jane.

Timothy glanced around quickly. "Yes!! She's looking all around—like she's hunting for somebody in the crowd. Probably us!"

Thinking quickly, Timothy spoke to Joey, the bored boy behind the table. "Somebody's following my cousins and me. Can we hide under your table?"

"OK with me," said Joey. "It's nice to have some *excitement* around here for a change. I'll be

your lookout.''

Titus and Sarah-Jane crawled under the table. The tablecloth reached all the way to the floor. It made a perfect hiding place.

Timothy didn't want to make any sudden moves. He waited casually while Joey put his buttons in a bag and gave him the change. Then, when he saw that the woman had her back to him, he dropped down and crawled under the table to join his cousins in hiding.

6
THE CAT'S SECRET

Joey's voice came quietly from above the table.
"Who am I on the lookout *for*?" he asked.

"The lady with the pink-checked blouse,"
Timothy answered just as quietly.

"OK, here's the plan," said Joey. He sounded
happy and excited. "If I knock *once* on the table,
it just means I Have to Tell You Something. If I
knock *twice*, it means Freeze! Danger! And if I
knock *three* times, it means All Clear. Now,
knock back once if you understand."

Timothy reached up and knocked once on the
underside of the table, which was the roof of their
hiding place.

The cousins settled down to wait for the All
Clear.

Joey knocked once from above. "The lady is

talking to a man in a green-striped shirt. Is he after you, too?"

"Not that we know of," said Timothy. "But keep us posted."

Timothy turned to his cousins. "It still beats me why she wants that cat so much."

All three of them looked at the cat. It *did* seem to be laughing to itself—as if maybe it knew a secret.

Sarah-Jane said, "Hey. I almost forgot. As long as we're waiting, I'll take the change out."

She pulled hard on the black rubber stopper. It popped out, and a little pile of coins tumbled into her lap.

The cousins stared at the coins. There were no quarters. No dimes. No nickels. And no pennies. In fact, the coins didn't look like any they had ever seen before.

Titus looked seriously at Timothy and Sarah-Jane. "Are you thinking what I'm thinking?" he asked.

Timothy started to say, "No, what?" But then he stopped. "Ti!" he whispered excitedly. "Are you thinking these are the *rare coins* that were stolen this morning?"

Titus nodded. "Yep. That's exactly what I'm thinking."

"But how did the coins get in my cat bank?" Sarah-Jane asked. "Wait a minute! The table where I bought my cat is right next to the coin table, right? Suppose somebody stole the coins—and had to find a good hiding place in a hurry? A cat bank would be a really good hiding place!"

"Yes," said Titus. "An EXcellent hiding place. All the thief would have to do is wait a little while. Then he could come back and buy the cat like a regular customer. I think that's why that

28

lady wants your cat so much, S-J. It's not really the *cat* she wants. It's the *rare coins* inside it!"

"Do you think she stole the coins in the first place?" asked Timothy.

"Maybe," said Titus. "Or maybe she's *helping* the person who stole them. What do you call someone who helps the bad guy?"

Sarah-Jane thought a moment. "An accomplice," she said.

"Right, an accomplice," said Titus. "Maybe she's an accomplice."

"Well," said Timothy, "no matter who stole the coins, we have to get them back to the dealer. We have to tell the police and our parents what happened."

"Yes," said Sarah-Jane. "We'll go as soon as we get the All Clear from Joey up there. But what if the lady sees us anyway? Maybe we should hide the coins someplace else. That way, even if she steals my cat, she won't get the dealer's rare coins."

Titus frowned thoughtfully. "It's a good idea to hide the coins someplace else, S-J. But she'll know right away the coins are gone—she won't

29

hear them jingling inside the cat.''

Timothy and Sarah-Jane had to agree that Titus was right. So the three of them sat and thought about the problem. Suddenly Timothy said, ''I know! We could use our own money! I mean, we'll put our own change in the cat bank to make it jingle.''

Quickly and quietly Timothy and Titus put their change inside the cat bank. (Sarah-Jane didn't have any change left from buying her cat.) Then Sarah-Jane put the stopper back in the bank.

The cousins decided that Sarah-Jane should

still be in charge of the cat, since it belonged to her. And they decided that Timothy and Titus should be in charge of the rare coins. The boys split the coins up and hid them deep inside their pockets.

"Good work," said Timothy. "Now we just have to wait for the All Clear."

Just then Joey knocked. But it was *two* knocks—for DANGER!

8
THE ACCOMPLICE AND THE THIEF

The cousins froze. Trying not to make a sound. Trying not even to *breathe*.

There were many different footsteps and voices from the aisle on the other side of the tablecloth. But the cousins could hear one voice they recognized. The young woman who was following them.

"Those kids were right here the last time I saw them," she said. "And they still had the cat."

"I just hope they haven't looked inside the cat!" said a man's voice. "Keep searching for them. I have to get back to the coin table now. The old man will wonder why I'm taking such a long break."

The footsteps of the man and the woman moved away in opposite directions.

Soon Joey gave three knocks for All Clear.

Timothy, Titus, and Sarah-Jane heaved a sigh of relief.

"That was close!" said Titus. "But at least we know who the thief is."

"The man with the green-striped shirt," said Sarah-Jane.

"Yes, the coin dealer's assistant," said Timothy.

9
HELP! POLICE!

The cousins crawled out from under the table. "Thanks, Joey!" they said.

"Anytime," Joey replied. "That sure was more fun than selling buttons!"

The cousins saw the woman—the accomplice—farther up the side aisle. She was walking away from them, but they couldn't get to their *parents* without going past her.

Across the other side aisle they could see the coin dealer's assistant—the thief. He was waiting on customers at the coin table. But the cousins couldn't get to the *police* without going past *him*.

"What should we do?" asked Sarah-Jane.

"The comic books!" said Titus.

"Ti!" said Timothy impatiently. "This is no time to be thinking about comic books!"

"No," said Titus. "I meant, look at the comic books corner. The coin dealer is walking by there. Maybe he's taking a break and stretching his legs. I think we can get over to him. Then we can explain everything."

They started off quietly and carefully, trying not to be seen.

But it was no good.

The assistant spotted them.

He waved to his accomplice from across the room.

The young woman turned around and hurried after Timothy, Titus, and Sarah-Jane.

The cousins had just reached the coin dealer. They were trying to explain everything to him when the woman swept past them around the corner. She snatched the cat right out of Sarah-Jane's hands and continued up the aisle toward the coin table.

"My cat!" cried Sarah-Jane.

The cat saleslady looked up from her table and saw what happened.

"Help! Help! Police!" she yelled. "THAT WOMAN STOLE THAT LITTLE GIRL'S

CAT!''

The police hurried down the aisle to see what was wrong.

''I am so sick of this stupid cat!'' cried the woman to the dealer's assistant. ''Here—*you* take it!'' She tossed the cat to him. He tried to catch it, but he missed. The cat fell to the floor and smashed into a hundred pieces.

The woman tried to run away, but the police stopped her.

The dealer's assistant ran to the broken cat and began digging through the pieces.

''What are you looking for?'' asked the policeman suspiciously.

''He's looking for these, Officer,'' said Timothy. He and Titus dug deep into their pockets and brought out the rare coins.

"*My coins*!" cried the old dealer. He looked both angry and sad as he turned to his assistant. "So *you're* the thief! I trusted you. And you stole my coins. You hid them in that china cat. And then what? Your friend was supposed to come along and buy the cat?"

The assistant scowled. "I figured the coins were *safe* in that cat. It's so funny looking, I never thought anyone else would buy it."

"Humph!" said the saleslady.

"Oh, my poor kitty!" said Sarah-Jane. She tried to hold back the tears, but she couldn't.

"Don't cry, S-J," said Timothy and Titus together. They stooped down and picked out their change from the broken pieces. "Look, we still have some change from our 'mad money.' You

can have it to buy something else.''

But the old dealer said, ''That's very nice of you boys. Very generous. It's good to see some-one sharing instead of stealing. But the cat got broken because you tried to help me, so . . .'' He turned to Sarah-Jane. ''Pick out anything you like, my girl, and I will buy it for you.''

Sarah-Jane went straight to the table where she had bought the cat. Timothy and Titus looked at each other and shrugged. They *still* didn't see anything they liked there.

Sarah-Jane picked out the pink china flamingo

figurine. "I almost got the flamingo in the first place," she explained. Then she shook it to make sure there weren't any stolen coins in it. Everybody laughed. Everybody, that is, except the thief and his accomplice.

"You kids did some great detective work!" said the policemen.

The cousins would have liked to stay and hear more about that. But Titus said, "Oh, wow! Look at the time! It's going on two o'clock."

"We'd better get back to the antique furniture," said Timothy.

As they hurried along, Sarah-Jane said, "Tell you what, Tim and Ti. Today could be the beginning of the T.C.D.C."

"What's a 'teesy-deesy'?" asked Timothy and Titus.

"No, no, no," said Sarah-Jane. "I meant, Capital T.
Capital C.
Capital D.
Capital C.
It stands for the Three Cousins Detective Club."

"Hey, neat-O!" said Timothy.

"EXcellent," said Titus.

They were panting by the time they skidded up to their parents. But they were right on time.

Sarah-Jane's father looked up from the dresser drawer he was examining. He said, "Well, hello, you three. Did you have a high old time at the flea market?"

Timothy and Titus looked at each other and grinned. "Well, you could say that, Uncle Art!"

"Oh, Daddy!" said Sarah-Jane. "Just wait till you hear!"

The End

THE TEN COMMANDMENTS MYSTERIES

When Timothy, Titus, and Sarah-Jane, the three cousins, get together the most ordinary events turn into mysteries. So they've formed the T.C.D.C. (That's the Three Cousins Detective Club.)

And while the three cousins are solving mysteries, they're also learning about the Ten Commandments and living God's way.

You'll want to solve all ten mysteries along with Sarah-Jane, Ti, and Tim:

The Mystery of the Laughing Cat—"You shall not steal." *Someone stole rare coins. Can the cousins find the thief?*

The Mystery of the Messed-up Wedding—"You shall not commit adultery." *Can the cousins find the missing wedding ring?*

The Mystery of the Gravestone Riddle—"You shall not murder." *Can the cousins solve a 100-year-old murder case?*

The Mystery of the Carousel Horse—"You shall not covet." *Why does the stranger want an old, wooden horse?*

The Mystery of the Vanishing Present—"Remember the Sabbath day and keep it holy." *Can the cousins figure out who has Grandpa's missing birthday gift?*

The Mystery of the Silver Dolphin—"You shall not give false testimony." *Who's telling the truth—and who's lying?*

The Mystery of the Tattletale Parrot—"You shall not misuse the name of the Lord your God." *What will the beautiful green parrot say next?*

The Mystery of the Second Map—"You shall have no other gods before me." *Can the cousins discover who dropped the strange map?*

The Mystery of the Double Trouble—"Honor your father and your mother." *How could Timothy be in two places at once?*

The Mystery of the Silent Idol—"You shall not make for yourself an idol." *If the idol could speak, what would it tell the cousins?*

Available at your local Christian bookstore.

David C. Cook Publishing Co., Elgin, IL 60120

THE KIDS FROM
APPLE STREET CHURCH

How did it happen?

Every day brings new excitement in the lives of Mary Jo, Danny, and the other kids from Apple Street Church. Whether it's finding a stolen doll in a coat sleeve, chasing important papers all over the school yard, meeting a famous astronaut, or discovering the real truth about a mysteriously broken leg, the kids write it all in their personal notebooks to God.

Usually diaries are private. But this is your chance to look over the shoulders of The Kids from Apple Street Church as they tell God about their secret thoughts, their problems, and their fun times. It's just like praying, except they are writing to God instead of talking to Him.

Don't miss any of the adventures of The Kids from Apple Street Church!

1. Mary Jo Bennett
2. Danny Petrowski
3. Julie Chang
4. Pug McConnell
5. Becky Garcia
6. Curtis Anderson

Available at your local Christian bookstore.

David C. Cook Publishing Co.
850 N. Grove Ave.
Elgin, IL 60120

Chariot Books

SHOELACES AND BRUSSELS SPROUTS

One little lie, but BIG trouble!

When Alex lies to her mom about losing her shoelaces, it doesn't seem like a big deal. But how do you replace special baseball laces when you don't have any money and you're not allowed to go to the store alone? A big softball game is coming up, and Alex knows the coach won't let her pitch in shoes without laces—or in cowboy boots!

Every kid gets into the predicaments that Alex does—ones that start out small and mushroom. Readers will learn from Alex's mistakes and understand that they have the same sources of help that she turns to: A God who loves them and wants to help them, and parents who understand.

Other books in the Alex Series . . .

2 *French Fry Forgiveness*—Sometimes making friends is harder than making enemies.

3 *Hot Chocolate Friendship*—Is winning first place as important to Alex as being a friend?

4 *Peanut Butter and Jelly Secrets*—Obeying her parents (even in little things) beats the awful results of disobeying.

Available at your local Christian bookstore.

David C. Cook Publishing Co.
850 N. Grove Ave.
Elgin, IL 60120

Chariot Books

If you liked this book, you'll also want to solve all the Beatitudes Mysteries along with Sarah-Jane, Titus, and Timothy:

The Mystery of the Empty School
"Blessed are the meek"
The Mystery of the Candy Box
"Blessed are the merciful"
The Mystery of the Disappearing Papers
"Blessed are the pure in heart"
The Mystery of the Secret Snowman
"Blessed are the peacemakers"
The Mystery of the Golden Pelican
"Blessed are those who mourn"
The Mystery of the Princess Doll
"Blessed are those who are persecuted"
The Mystery of the Hidden Egg
"Blessed are the poor in spirit"
The Mystery of the Clumsy Juggler
"Blessed are those who hunger and thirst for righteousness"